SANTA
DOG

Coming Soon!

SANTA DOG

By Marcia Thornton Jones and Debbie Dadey

Illustrated by Amy Wummer

Hyperion Books for Children
New York

To Justin, Christina, and Sean Pellman, great
neighbors   —DD

To those who make the holiday season special,
including my family—and, of course, Santa Claus!
                                                    —MTJ

Printed in the United States of America
First Edition
1 3 5 7 9 10 8 6 4 2
Book design by Dawn Adelman
This book is set in 14-pt. Cheltenham.
ISBN 0-7868-1677-5
Visit www.barkleyschool.com

Contents

MAGIC STUFF

"This is fang-tastic!" Bubba the pup shouted.

I, Jack, the Wonder Dog, had to admit he was right. Snow covered everything in sight, turning the back of our school into a winter playground. Barkley's School for Dogs is like most schools, only it's for dogs—not kids. Instead of swings, we have tunnels to run through and bars to jump over. Snow sparkled on everything. I decided to share some of my wisdom with Bubba. "This is magic stuff," I told him. "It's Christmas snow."

"Christmas?" Bubba asked. "What's that?"

I was ready with an answer, but a loud noise stopped me. *BANG! BANG! BANG!*

Bubba jumped behind me, and I hunkered, peering over my shoulder. When I figured out what was happening, I snickered a bit. "It's okay," I told Bubba. "Fred's hanging Christmas lights."

Bubba's little body scooted out from behind me to watch Fred Barkley, the human who ran Barkley's School for Dogs. Fred stood on a ladder, hammering nails into the side of the school. Then he hung twinkling lights from the nails. Pretty soon, the whole play yard sparkled with lights.

"Christmas really must be magic," Bubba whispered.

"Christmas is dog-awesome," I told him. "Humans sing songs, and make yummy treats, and Santa brings presents for everyone—even dogs!"

"Treats?" Bubba yipped. "Presents? I want treats and presents. Christmas sounds like the best time of year!"

I nodded, glad to share my Wonder Dog wisdom. Maybe it's the snow or the lights, but something about Christmas always makes me feel warm and fuzzy inside.

That nice warm feeling suddenly chilled when Sweetcakes jumped right in front of Bubba and me. Sweetcakes sent

snow flying everywhere with her pounce. Snow splattered Bubba and me from our black noses to the tips of our shaggy tails. Bubba and I gulped. Sweetcakes was not your Christmas kind of dog. She was the meanest Doberman pinscher this side of the North Pole, and she had the scars to prove it.

"Don't go getting your tails all a-wagging," Sweetcakes snarled. "Santa isn't going to bring you presents."

"He won't?" Bubba asked, looking very sad.

Sweetcakes grinned an evil grin. "No," she snapped, "only puppies believe in Santa."

"Yeah, yeah," Clyde said. "Puppies." The stubby bulldog always followed Sweetcakes. He also repeated everything she said.

"That's not true," I said, looking Sweetcakes right in the eye. "Of course Santa is real."

Sweetcakes got so close to me I could feel her hot breath on my face. I didn't know what would happen next, but I feared I would never see Christmas again.

DOG-HONEST TRUTH

"I believe in Santa," a familiar voice yipped.

It was Blondie. Her curly white poodle hair blended in with the snow blanketing the play yard. Blondie was not only the prettiest dog I'd ever met, she was also the nicest.

Blondie wasn't alone. My good buddies, Woodrow and Floyd, were at her side.

Blondie marched right up to Sweet-cakes and faced her nose-to-nose. "Stop

teasing Bubba," she told Sweetcakes.

"Every dog knows Santa Claus is real," Floyd said. Floyd was hard to understand, since he liked to chew on things. Today, he had a squeaking rubber reindeer clamped in his beagle jaws.

"He is as nice to dogs and cats as he is to kids," Woodrow added. I looked over at Woodrow. His forehead wrinkled in seriousness. Woodrow was the smartest dog in the yard. If he said Santa was real, it was the dog-honest truth.

I grinned at Sweetcakes. "You can't ruin our Christmas spirit," I told her.

"It's not Christmas yet," Sweetcakes snarled. "I have plenty of time. Besides, the only dog around here that's going to get treats and presents is me. I get them ALL!" Sweetcakes stomped off, spraying snow all over Clyde as he hurried to follow.

I looked at my friends. They stared after Sweetcakes. Woodrow's ears dragged in the snow. Floyd was so upset he had chewed a hole in his new toy. Bubba's tail had stopped wagging and was lying flat in the snow.

I knew all about Christmas from my human, Maggie. Christmas was Maggie's favorite time of year. I had to set the record straight. "Christmas is no time to worry about bullies. We have to think about all those presents," I said in my smartest voice. "Surprises hidden in packages and wrapped with bows."

"Don't forget about decorations," Blondie added, a little smile coming back to her eyes.

I nodded. "Maggie takes decorating very seriously. Every year, her school decorates the tree in the park for everyone to enjoy."

"Do we get to help?" Bubba asked.

I shook my head with Wonder Dog wisdom. "Maggie works and works and works on her own decoration. This year I can tell her project is very special because she has been cutting and pasting and stitching for days. She even helps decorate a tree in our apartment."

"An indoor tree?" Bubba asked, the tip of his tail getting a little twitchy. "A tree with branches?"

"That's right," I said. "And Christmas is about treats, too." I licked my chops as I remembered the smells and tastes of Christmas. "And Maggie stays home from her school, which means she can spend more time with me."

Floyd tossed his rubber reindeer in the air and caught it. "Toys! I hope I get lots of chew toys!"

"I can't wait," Bubba said. Sweetcakes was long forgotten. Bubba's tail wagged so hard the little guy's entire body wiggled.

The only dog who hadn't cheered up was Woodrow. He sighed. "I can wait. Christmas makes me tired," he said. "All those visiting kids tug my ears and try to smooth out my forehead. It gives me a headache."

"I like it when people pet my head," Floyd said. "My human takes me on a long car ride and scratches my ears. That's my favorite part of Christmas. Sometimes he lets me poke my nose out the window. The smells are great. Great. GREAT!" Floyd wagged his tail. He got so excited he dropped his chew toy and started howling.

"I'll be down soon!" Fred Barkley yelled from atop his ladder. "Try to stay quiet!"

Floyd's mouth snapped shut and his eyes opened wide. Lights already twinkled from the building. Now Fred was draping lights along the brick wall that surrounded our play yard.

Sweetcakes sat at the base of Fred's ladder and looked our way. "Mark my words," Sweetcakes said. "You dogs are getting excited over absolutely, positively, nothing!"

"Yeah, yeah," Clyde repeated from his place under the ladder. "Nothing."

"Take it from me," I told all my friends as soon as I was sure Sweetcakes had her ragged ears turned in another direction. "Don't listen to a thing Sweetcakes has to say. Christmas is a dog-awesome time, so don't let Sweetcakes spoil it!"

NAUGHTY OR NICE?

Christmas was coming, that was sure. I could tell. Maggie slept late, so that meant she didn't have to go to school. I sniffed under the decorated tree that stood in the corner of the room. I pushed a few packages aside, rooting for one that might be for me. I stopped when Maggie yelled, "No, Jack!" I guess she didn't want me to find my present before the big day.

Maggie is the sweetest human on this earth, but when she yells at me, it hurts me down to my paws. Luckily, she doesn't stay mad for long. Maggie jingled my leash. "Today is going to be a fun day," she told me. "I'm going to school with you!"

I licked every one of her fingers. Any day with Maggie was bound to be fun. I couldn't wait to get started. As soon as she opened the door to our apartment, I scrambled into the hall, pulling Maggie behind me. Unfortunately, Miss Frimple, our neighbor across the hall, stepped

in the way. Her cat, Tazz, was peeking out the open door. Tazz was no stranger to me. Tazz had a habit of getting on my nerves. "Are you causing trouble again?" Tazz meowed in cat talk.

I barked back, "No!" It wasn't my fault that my leash got wrapped around Miss Frimple's ankles.

"That mutt is trying to break my leg," Miss Frimple screeched in a voice that

traveled six city blocks. It was a known fact that she didn't like dogs.

"I'm sorry," Maggie said. Maggie's voice was as soft and sweet as caramel compared to Miss Frimple's. "Jack didn't mean to trip you."

"That dog," Miss Frimple said, "is the naughtiest animal in this entire neighborhood."

"He didn't mean it," Maggie said, inching down the hall. "I'll make him be nice from now on."

I cocked my ears. What could Maggie be talking about? I was the nicest dog in town. As we hurried through the door, the last thing I heard was enough to make me growl. Tazz was laughing at me.

Maggie didn't talk to me the whole way to school. We must have been a little late, because all the other dogs were clustered in the front office. Fred stood at the front of the room, his hands full of leashes. A few other dogs huddled by their humans' feet.

I looked for my friends. Floyd chewed on his toy, and Blondie pranced near the front of the line. Woodrow sat by the door. He sighed when he saw me.

"What's going on?" I asked Woodrow.

"We're going on a field trip," Woodrow said with a yawn. "Which means I'm going to miss my nap." Woodrow's favorite hobby was napping.

Bubba hopped in front of my nose. "It's a trip to the park," he yelped. "There's a brand-new spot made just for dogs. We get to run and play and meet other dogs. Is this because of Christmas?"

I gave the little pup a nudge. "This is part of Christmas magic," I explained. "Our humans take more time to do fun things."

Just then, Fred cleared his throat. "Before we leave," he said, "let's go over a few rules."

I scratched at an ear and yawned. I didn't really need to listen to this. After all, a Wonder Dog knows all the rules. Fred, however, seemed a little confused. He looked straight at me as he counted out directions on his fingers. "No barking. No fighting. Stay together."

Sweetcakes stood at Fred's side. She glared at me and raised a lip over her jagged tooth in a snarl. "Watch me, and I'll

show you how to behave like a champ," she said.

"Yeah, Champ," Clyde muttered.

"A champion grouch," I said with a low growl. The words were out of my mouth before I had a chance to swallow them.

Maggie kneeled beside me. "Behave, Jack." I reached over and licked her nose. Maggie didn't have to worry about me. In fact, there was nothing to worry about.

But with Sweetcakes around, I should have known better.

JiNGLES

"Why did Maggie say that?" Bubba asked as we made our way to the nearby park. "You always behave."

I smiled at the little pup. "Thank you, Bubba. But everyone knows you have to be especially good before Christmas," I explained, "since Santa only gives presents if you're good."

"Then I'm going to be better than good," Bubba said as we got close to the park, "because I want toys, toys, toys!"

My nose started working overtime the

closer we got to the park. Trees. Bushes. Shoes. Boots. There were so many things to sniff. Maggie obviously couldn't keep up with my Wonder Dog nose, and she tugged at my leash. I would do anything in the world for Maggie, but sometimes she moves a little on the slow side. I guess that's because she only has two legs instead of four.

In the middle of the park was a brand-new dog run. Fred led us to the gate.

"Now, remember what I told you," he said.

Sweetcakes stood next to Fred. The hair on her back stood up a good inch, and she raised a lip over one yellow fang. "Behave," she snarled just loud enough for me to hear, "or else."

"Or else what?" I asked without even thinking.

"This will be the worst Christmas of your life," Sweetcakes warned.

Her low growl turned my stomach to ice. Sweetcakes was trying her dog-best to ruin my Christmas spirit. I couldn't let her do that. I was about to put her in her place, once and for all. Really, I was. But just then, Fred opened the gate.

I squeezed between two Irish setters, Rhett and Scarlett, in order to beat most of the dogs. As soon as we were inside the dog run, Maggie unsnapped my leash. Free! I was free!

The first thing I did was run to a tree and sniff.

Then I saw a snow-covered bush and darted straight for it. I had to jump over little Petey. Petey was a terrier, and digging is what he does best. He was so busy digging in the snow, he didn't notice when I sailed over him. Maggie didn't jump over him, though. She was getting farther and farther behind. "Hurry, hurry, hurry!" I barked to anyone who listened.

"What? What? What?" Floyd answered.

"Where? Where? Where?" Bubba answered with his puppy howl.

Pretty soon, all the dogs were barking and racing after me.

I didn't have time to slow down. I had to reach that bush before all my buddies. I hurried to sniff the bush. That's when I noticed the warm smell of another dog. This was no ordinary dog scent. There was something else mixed in with it. Then it hit me. It smelled like the red-and-white candy canes Maggie hung from our Christmas tree. Peppermint!

Peppermint made my nose tingle. I wanted some of that candy. I had to find the mystery dog before anyone else did.

I dashed across the dog area so fast that I felt snow flying behind me.

I raced so fast, I almost missed the peppermint-scented dog. That's because his white furry coat blended in with the snow. He wore a red-and-white-striped collar with a bell around his neck.

I skidded to a stop just in time. "I'm Jack," I panted. "I've been looking all over for you."

The big American Eskimo dog reached out his huge paw. "My name is Jingles," he said. Sure enough, his collar even jingled.

I puffed out my chest just a little. Being a Wonder Dog, I wanted to be friendly to the new dog.

Bubba and Floyd galloped up before I had a chance to say another word. Blondie, Rhett, and Scarlett weren't far behind. Woodrow was taking his time. Of course, all the dogs moved out of the way when Sweetcakes sauntered into the pack.

"So, you're the new dog in town," Sweetcakes said, sniffing the little bell hanging from Jingles's collar. Sweetcakes asked the new dog, "Where are your humans?"

Jingles smiled. "I'm not really new. I've visited before. I live farther north, but my humans do a lot of traveling this time of year. In fact, they're preparing for their biggest trip of the year right now."

Bubba sat right under Jingles's chin and stared up at the fellow. The more Jingles talked, the more Bubba's ears perked up. I wondered what the little pup was thinking.

"Just be sure not to get in my way," Sweetcakes warned Jingles.

"Way, way," Clyde mumbled from Sweetcakes's shadow.

Jingles didn't look the least bit concerned. In fact, he grinned. "Oh, don't worry," he said. "I won't at all."

Obviously, Jingles didn't know Sweetcakes the way I did. I had to warn the new guy before it was too late.

SANTA'S DOG

"I've been thinking," Bubba told me.

"That's nice," I told him, opening my sleepy eyelids. We were back at Barkley's School for Dogs, and Fred had brought us inside to warm up. It was the dog-honest truth that I was plenty tired from all my running at the park. I definitely needed a nap.

Bubba nipped me on the nose. He did it gently, but it still stung. "Hey, what's the big idea?" I asked him.

"Sorry," Bubba said, "but I have something important to say."

I sighed and yawned so wide I was sure all my gleaming white teeth showed. Obviously, Bubba wasn't going to let me sleep until I heard what he had to say. Puppies are like that. "Okay, what's so important?" I asked.

"Jingles," Bubba said.

I nodded. "He seems like a nice enough dog." I liked Jingles. In fact, I planned to warn him about Sweetcakes the next time we saw him at the dog run.

"He's not an ordinary dog," Bubba explained.

"I noticed that, too," Floyd said, coming up beside Bubba. "There's something very different about that Eskimo dog."

"That's what I've been trying to say." Bubba jumped up and down. "I know what it is! I know!"

"What?" I asked, not really caring. All I wanted to do was take a nap. I guess maybe I did sound a little grumpy.

"Hear the puppy out," Woodrow suggested as he and Blondie made their way to the group.

"Be nice," Blondie added.

It was obvious I wasn't going to get my nap. I sat up and stretched. "Go on, then," I said. "What's different about Jingles?"

"I've listened to you and all the other dogs talk about Santa and Christmas," Bubba said. "I figured it out. Jingles's human is Santa Claus!" he yipped.

"That's it!" Floyd said. He bounced up and down beside Bubba. "We've found Santa's dog!"

All that bouncing made me dizzy. "Wait just a dog-gone minute," I said. "That's the craziest thing I've ever heard."

"Think about it," Bubba said. "Jingles is from up north and smells like peppermint. His humans travel around a lot—during Christmas!"

I had to admit, my Wonder Dog curiosity was starting to stir. I shook my head. That was crazy talk. Santa lived in the North Pole. I knew from Maggie that was far away. Santa couldn't be around here. Could he?

I didn't have time to think it all through because Sweetcakes nosed her way into our group. "Did I hear you talk about Santa again?" she asked.

"No," Bubba said before I could stop him. "We were talking about Santa Dog!"

Sweetcakes peered down at the pup and laughed. "There is no such thing as Santa Dog."

"That's not true," Floyd blurted. "Jingles is Santa Dog."

"We're going to find him when we go back to the park," Bubba added. "I plan to tell Santa Dog about the presents I want for Christmas."

Sweetcakes laughed out loud. "What

makes you think you will be allowed back in the dog run?" she asked.

Bubba stopped wagging his tail. "The dog run belongs to all of us, doesn't it?"

"That dog run is only for dogs who can *behave*," Sweetcakes said. She looked at me when she said it. "Fred saw for himself that I am the only dog at Barkley's worthy of using the dog run."

"The dog run is for us to share," I said.

"So dogs can play and have fun together," Woodrow added.

"I would never want to play and have fun with any of you," Sweetcakes said as she turned her tail to us.

As Sweetcakes walked away, Bubba sniffed. "How will I get to see Santa Dog if we never go back to the dog run?" he asked. "Christmas is going to be ruined!"

"Don't worry about a thing," I told the little fellow. "Sweetcakes can't ruin our Christmas. I'll see to that!"

A LiTTLE BiT OF KiNDNESS

I thought about Jingles before I went to sleep that night. What if he really was visiting from the North Pole? What was he doing in our town? In the morning it was all I could think about. With all that thinking going on, it was no wonder I didn't see where I was going when Maggie and I left for school.

Smack! I ran right into Miss Frimple in the hallway.

"I'm so sorry," Maggie apologized.

I was sorry, too. I even gave Miss

Frimple a lick on the leg, but she wasn't impressed. She grabbed a tissue out of her purse and scrubbed at her knee. "There is nothing worse than dog slobber!" she screeched.

"You forgot your mittens," Maggie's mom called from the front door. Maggie tied my leash to the stoop and told me to sit.

"Dogs are sooooo clumsy," Miss Frimple's cat, Tazz, purred to me. Tazz had followed Maggie and me out of the door. Just what I needed. A busybody cat to get in the way.

"I was thinking," I told Tazz. "I didn't see where I was going."

"A dog thinking?" Tazz teased. "I didn't know that was possible."

I would have growled, but I focused on Jingles instead. "Do you know anything about Santa?" I asked Tazz.

Tazz paused a minute to preen her paw before answering. "Sure, I've heard about Santa," Tazz said. "He's jolly and gives out presents."

"That's the one," I said. "Do you think he has a dog?"

Tazz acted like she was spitting up fur balls. "Are you kidding? Santa is too smart. He wouldn't want a dog. I'm sure he'd prefer a cat."

Obviously, Tazz would not be any help. Maybe Woodrow would know the answer. I was glad to see Maggie come back

outside. I wanted to get to school. I had some questions for Woodrow.

At school, Woodrow was in his usual place: a comfy pile of rags by the back door. "Do you really think Santa can be Jingles's human?" I asked him.

Woodrow lifted his head up from his nap and nodded. "There's no reason why he couldn't."

That made sense to me, but I still wasn't convinced. I had to talk to Jingles

again, but how could that happen? Jingles was at the park, and I was at Barkley's School for Dogs. And if Sweetcakes had any say in the matter, I wouldn't be setting my paws in the dog run for a long, long time. Sweetcakes thought she ruled the dog run, too.

For once, I was glad Fred Barkley could not understand dogspeak. Fred was pretty smart—for a human; but he still hadn't figured out how to understand our barks. Usually, that drove me crazy. Today I was glad.

"Okay, dogs," Fred said when he came out into the play yard. Leashes were draped over his shoulder. "Let's celebrate the season with another trip to the park."

Fred didn't see Sweetcakes trot up behind him.

"No!" Sweetcakes barked.

"No!" Clyde repeated.

Fred jumped around. "Sweetcakes!" he

yelled. "You scared me. You shouldn't bark like that!"

"These dogs can't go to the park," Sweetcakes said, barking even louder. "They can't, can't, CAN'T GO!"

Fred put his hands on his hips and glared at Sweetcakes. "Why are you barking?" he asked. "You know better than to make all that noise."

"I won't share with them!" Sweetcakes

barked. And this time, there was a healthy dose of growl mixed in. It was then I realized that Sweetcakes wanted the dog run for herself.

Fred took a step back. Then he leaned down to Sweetcakes and said the one word all dogs dread. "NO!"

Blondie gasped. Bubba whined. Floyd chewed his toy extra hard. Me? Well, I hate to admit it, but I giggled. I shouldn't have, but I did.

Sweetcakes glared at me. "I'll get you for this," she snarled.

I felt the hair on my back stiffen. I tensed, ready to take the force of Sweetcakes's pounce.

Bubba jumped in front of me just as Sweetcakes made her move.

THE REAL SPIRIT

"We have to be good," Bubba barked in his loudest puppy voice as Sweetcakes tensed her muscles to jump. "No fighting! No fighting!"

Fred turned around to see what Bubba was yapping about. "I guess we're all a little excited about another field trip," Fred said.

"Bubba's right," Floyd said when Fred had walked away. At least, that's what I thought Floyd said. It sounded more like "Bubbles gight," because Floyd's entire chew toy was jammed in his mouth.

"If Santa finds out we're naughty, he won't bring us toys or treats," Bubba said.

I stepped away from Sweetcakes and the hair on my back smoothed down. "The pup has a point," I said.

Sweetcakes did not look convinced. "I'm the only one making points around here, and you better understand this one."

"We'll be good at the park," Bubba said as he backed up to hide between my two paws. "We have to be good, or Jingles might tell Santa on us."

Then Sweetcakes turned and walked away. Usually, Sweetcakes made me mad enough to growl. This time I didn't have a chance because Fred snapped a leash to my collar. The dog run! This was my chance to find out if Jingles was the one and only Santa Dog!

In less than ten minutes we were at the dog run in the park. I sniffed high and low for Jingles. No peppermint. Had Jingles already left for the North Pole? Was I too late?

"Wait just a minute," I howled. Yes, I definitely caught a whiff of peppermint in the air. I darted across the dog run, ignoring the cold air that flapped my ears. There, standing near a snow-covered tree, was Jingles.

"Ho, ho, hello," Jingles greeted me. Sprigs of holly stuck out of his collar and his peppermint scent smelled yummy.

"I'm glad you're here," I told Jingles. "I have to ask you something." I knew that the best way to get answers was to come right out and ask questions. I was going to ask, plain and simple, if he was Santa's dog.

"I'm glad you're here, too," Jingles said with a shake of his collar that made the tiny silver bell tinkle. "I've been watching you and your friends. I think there is something you should know."

"You do?" I asked as Bubba, Floyd, Blondie, and Woodrow came up beside me.

"It's about Christmas," Jingles continued. "My humans love Christmas and try to share Christmas magic with the whole world."

"Lots of people love Christmas," I told Jingles.

"Not everyone," Jingles said. "And there are some who find it hard to be kind and giving. They find it easier to be naughty than nice."

I thought about Sweetcakes. She was definitely the naughty type, even though she pretended to be nice for Fred. She should be hearing what Jingles had to say. Not me. I was much nicer than Sweetcakes. I couldn't quite figure out why Jingles kept looking at me when he should have been sniffing out Sweetcakes.

"Christmas is about being kind and giving," Jingles explained. "It's not just about getting treats and toys at all."

"That's not what I heard," Bubba said. I squirmed a little when he looked up at me. "You mean we should be giving things to others?"

Jingles nodded again, making gentle music with his bell.

"That's a wonderful idea," Woodrow said with a crooked smile. "We've been wasting our time worrying about getting presents. We should do nice things for our humans instead."

"And for each other," Floyd said with a grin. Then he reached over and lay his chew toy on the snow in front of Bubba. "I'll start by letting Bubba play with my reindeer."

"Planning nice things will be fun," Blondie said. Floyd, Woodrow, and Bubba agreed. They huddled close and started thinking of ways to be nice.

"That's the spirit," Jingles said, "the real spirit of the holiday. Of course, it's easiest to be nice to our friends. It's harder to be nice to those who haven't been friendly to us."

I wasn't sure about that part. I sat

down and scratched my ear to think it through. That's when I realized I still hadn't gotten to the bottom of who Jingles's human was. I turned around and opened my mouth to ask. I slapped my jaws shut. Jingles was gone.

"Where did that dog go?" I asked Bubba.

Bubba looked around. Dogs of every shape and size filled the dog run. "What dog?" Bubba asked.

"Jingles!" I said.

"I didn't see where he went," Floyd said.

"We were too busy planning nice things for Fred," Blondie added.

Woodrow looked around and shrugged. He didn't say a word, but someone else answered.

"Hey, doggie! Are you looking for that Eskimo pup?" Tazz called from outside the fence. She pranced along, swishing

her tail. No time is a good time for a cat, but I needed information fast.

"Which way did the white dog go?" I asked.

Tazz licked her paw before answering. "He went that way with a lady in a red coat." Tazz pointed toward the park entrance with her paw.

I looked over, but I couldn't see a thing. Jingles had left so suddenly—it was almost like he had disappeared!

CHRiSTMAS MAGiC

"My human was so happy," Blondie told me the next morning. "I let her sleep late."

"That's nice," I said as all my other friends gathered around. Fred had shoveled a path in the yard for us so we didn't have to stand in the snow.

Floyd dropped his rubber reindeer and panted. "I fetched my human's slippers. He was so tickled he gave me a good belly rub."

"I gave my human his paper, and I didn't

even drool on it," Woodrow said proudly.

It seemed like all the dogs had been treating their humans extra nice, except me. I felt a little guilty. I hadn't thought of anything for Maggie yet.

"This is Christmas magic!" Bubba bounced around in front of me. "It's exactly what Santa Dog was telling us about. The Christmas magic is making us be nice."

I shook my head. "I wouldn't be so sure about that."

But Bubba was certain. "It is," he said firmly. "And I know where all the magic came from."

"Where?" Blondie asked after licking a delicate white paw.

"Jingles," Bubba announced. "He's Santa's dog, and he's magic."

Floyd nodded, his ears drooping into the snow. "That makes sense to me."

"We still don't know that Jingles's human is Santa," I told my friends.

Bubba didn't listen to me, he was too excited. "Not only that, but maybe we'll get to see Santa tonight!"

"Santa is here?" I asked.

Floyd barked. "He'll probably be at the tree-lighting ceremony at the park. My human's taking me. I can't wait to tell Jingles how good I've been. Maybe he'll tell Santa."

I felt a strange tingle in my tail. I knew Maggie had been working on her special decoration all week. She wouldn't miss the ceremony, and I knew she would bring me along. I closed my eyes and tried to imagine the crisp air, the twinkling lights, walking proudly by Maggie's side up to the giant park tree and putting her special decoration in a place.

A growl interrupted my daydream. Sweetcakes. "You better not be there," she warned. "I don't want you or any

other mutt to ruin the ceremony for Fred."

"Don't worry about me," I said. "I never cause trouble."

"Just see that you don't," Sweetcakes said before marching away.

"Poor Sweetcakes," Floyd said softly.

"Poor Sweetcakes, my tail," I sputtered. "She's been trying to ruin our Christmas spirit all week!"

"That's exactly why we should be nice to her," Floyd said with a worried look.

I couldn't believe my good friend was sticking up for a dog whose heart was colder than snow.

"That's what Christmas is about," Woodrow said.

"Remember," Floyd said, "Jingles said we have to be nice to everyone."

"They're right," Blondie said gently. "*Everyone* includes Sweetcakes."

I sat down and gave my ear a thorough scratch. "What about Tazz?" I asked. "And Miss Frimple?"

"Everybody," Woodrow said softly.

It was hard enough thinking of special things for Maggie. How would I ever face being nice to Sweetcakes? Or Tazz? And, even Miss Frimple?

A WONDER DOG CAPE

Maggie jangled my leash, and I jumped up, gently placing my paws on her knees. There's no better music than the sound of Maggie's giggle. It made my tail wag extra fast, but my tail slowed when I realized Christmas was in a few days, and I still hadn't thought of something nice to do for her.

"Tonight is the night," Maggie told me. "We light the park tree. My decoration is all ready."

I followed Maggie into the big room.

There, folded on a table, was an extra-thick blanket. I knew Maggie had carefully cut out shapes from glittery paper and glued them on to make it pretty. She had even hand-stitched an edging of stars. "This tree skirt will complete the tree," Maggie told me. "I made it all by myself!"

Maggie had done something nice for everyone in the city by making the tree skirt, but I hadn't done a single thing for Maggie. What was I going to do?

Maggie zipped on her coat and slapped earmuffs over her ears. Then she grabbed my red Wonder Dog cape from the doggie bed. "It's going to be cold tonight," she said as she draped the cape around my back. I stood tall and proud. Everyone at the park would be impressed.

Maggie was being extra nice to me. I had to think of something for her.

Thinking and walking is hard to do. But

I set my mind to the task as we headed down the hall of our apartment building. We were almost to the front door, when I heard something that turned my stomach to icicles. Miss Frimple.

"Are you heading for the big celebration?" she called in that voice that made my ears hurt. She shut the door to her apartment, after Tazz slipped out and jumped in her arms. Miss Frimple hurried down the hallway after us. "I'll walk with you."

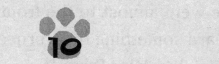

THiNK! THiNK! THiNK!

"You're late!" Blondie said when Maggie and I finally arrived at the park. Miss Frimple and Tazz were close behind.

My friends and their humans were clustered near the giant tree. Huge colorful ornaments hung from the branches and a star was perched at the tip-top. The scent of the pine needles tickled my nose.

"Did you make a decoration for the tree?" Miss Frimple asked.

"Yes." Maggie smiled. And then Maggie's face changed.

"What's wrong, dear?" Miss Frimple said.

"I forgot the tree skirt that I made!" Maggie looked very sad.

Miss Frimple patted Maggie's arm. "It's too late to get it now. I'm sure everything will be all right." Maggie still looked upset, so I licked her hand to make her feel better.

I wanted to tell my friends what had happened, but they didn't give me a chance.

"This has been great," Floyd said as

Maggie and I walked up. "We've been nice to everyone.

Woodrow's ears swayed when he nodded. A crooked smile creased his forehead even more. "I cuddled on my human's lap for twenty minutes to warm him up," he said. "I could tell it made his day."

Bubba hopped in front of me. "We

were even nice to Sweetcakes," he said. "Jingles's Christmas magic really works. Once you start it, the magic spreads on its own."

"Bubba might be right," Blondie said. "We saw Sweetcakes giving Fred a kiss on the cheek."

I gulped. This was serious. Sweetcakes is not a kissy kind of dog. She was more of a "bite you on the behind" kind of dog. Something strange was definitely going on. If there really was magic, I needed it now for Maggie. I had to find Jingles.

"Has anyone seen that Santa Dog?" I asked.

"He isn't anywhere," Bubba said. "We sniffed and sniffed, but the only peppermint we found was a gooey candy wrapper in a kid's hand."

I was out of time. The lighting of the special tree was about to begin. Only one thing was needed—the tree skirt.

Maggie sniffed and took a step forward. I knew she was getting ready to tell them she didn't have it.

Think! Think! Think! What could I do to help my Maggie?

Something tugged at my Wonder Dog cape. I looked down. There sat Tazz, one claw hooked into my thick cape.

"Not now, Tazz," I warned. "I have to think, think, think."

Tazz tugged my cape again, causing it to slip off my back. "Well, try not to hurt

that Blunder Dog brain of yours," she purred. "It's not used to thinking." Then, with a little snicker, she wound her way around several sets of human legs and disappeared.

When I tried to shake my cape back in place, I came up with a dog-awesome idea.

I nudged Maggie's hand. Then I licked her fingers. Finally I barked. Maggie kneeled beside me to scratch my ears. I took a little step until her hand fell on my Wonder Dog cape. Then I stared right into Maggie's eyes.

Maggie looked at me. I saw her blink back her tears. "Your cape!" she said. "I could use your cape!"

Maggie threw her arms around my neck. "You are the best dog in the world," Maggie whispered in my ear. She unhooked my Wonder Dog cape, and, gently, she wrapped it beneath the tree just as the lights were switched on. The tree sparkled and twinkled. It was a beautiful sight—and I got to share it with my friends.

"That was the nicest thing I've ever seen you do," Blondie said softly.

"It's Jingles's magic at work," Floyd said.

"Speaking of Jingles, where is that dog?" Woodrow asked. "He missed the whole thing."

"No, he didn't," Bubba said. "Listen."

Far in the distance, there was the sound of bells ringing. Only these bells weren't near the ground. They came from high overhead.

"Do you think it's Jingles?" Bubba asked. "In Santa's sleigh?"

I had to admit, I believed. "I think it is," I said. "I think it is."

Floyd sat on the ground, looking up to the sky and grinning. "Jingles taught us

that Christmas magic isn't about getting things."

Bubba nodded. "It's about giving!

I thought I heard a faint "Ho, ho, ho." I couldn't tell if it was someone in the crowd or from a red sleigh high above the park. But there was one thing I did know for dog-sure—this was the most magical Christmas ever.